MATCHING A DAWN GOD

A JINX PARANORMAL DATING AGENCY STORY

LAURA GREENWOOD

Visit Laura Greenwood's website at:

www.authorlauragreenwood.co.uk

Cover by Vampari Designs

Matching A Dawn God is a work of fiction. Names, characters, places, and incidents are the products of the author's imagination or are used fictitiously. Any resemblance to actual persons, living or dead, businesses, companies, events, or locales is entirely coincidental.

If you find an error, you can report it via my website. Please note that my books are written in British English: https://www. authorlauragreenwood.co.uk/p/report-error.html

To keep up to date with new releases, sales, and other updates, you can join my mailing list via my website or The Paranormal Council Reader Group on Facebook.

BLURB

Swiping right for a god could lead to more than this witch ever expected.

The last thing Anise expected when she signed up to a dating app was to match with a god, and yet now, she's found exactly that happening.

Kuk has no idea why he finds this witch so enchanting when he doesn't think that of the others, but there's something about Anise that he can't get out of his head.
Will the two of them take a chance on their match?
-

Matching A Dawn God is a mythology-inspired paranormal m/f romance and part of the Jinx Paranormal Dating Agency series. It features an Egyptian dawn & darkness god, and a bubbly witch seeking romance on a dating app.

If you enjoy light-hearted paranormal romances featuring gods from different mythologies around the world, a hint of steam, and a happy ever after at the end of every book, start the Jinx Paranormal Dating Agency series today!

A NOTE ON THE JINX PARANORMAL DATING AGENCY

The *Jinx Paranormal Dating Agency* series exists in a world where all of the pantheons that have ever existed co-exist. All gods/goddesses, demi-gods, and immortals have access to both the god realm and Earth, and can move between the two. Paranormals are able to travel to and through the god realm, but typically only when they're accompanied, or are invited, by a god.

You can find a list of all the deities mentioned in the series on my website: https://www.authorlauragreenwood.co.uk/p/god-list-to-date-god-series.html

The Main God in Matching A Dawn God:

Kuk is an Egyptian god of darkness (specifically before dawn), and obscurity.

ONE

Anise

THE BELL RANG as the door of The Coven Copy Shop opened and I found myself preparing to face the customer on the other side, even if my heart wasn't completely in it. Retail wasn't exactly my first calling, but until I finished night school, there was nothing I could do about it except put up with the situation and hope it would get better soon.

I relaxed the moment I recognised the handsome man walking into the shop. I wasn't needed for this particular interaction and for good reason. Chelsea straightened in her position at the till beside me, her gaze locking onto her favourite customer.

"Do you want to..." she trailed off, probably because she didn't want me to say I'd deal with him.

"All yours," I responded with amusement in my voice.

For a moment, I thought she was going to argue with me, or worse, try to convince me that she didn't have a mythical-sized crush on one of our best customers, but instead, she walked over to him with a bright smile on her face.

He returned the moment he realised she was helping him today. I let out a wistful sigh, wishing that someone was around to look at me that way. It wasn't even because Baal was hot, though that didn't help, it was the way he seemed completely enraptured by everything my friend did. He was clearly besotted even if she was refusing to see it.

My phone buzzed and I pulled it out despite being on shift. I knew I wasn't supposed to, but with Chelsea distracted and no one else in the shop, it didn't seem like there'd be any harm in it. I swiped open the screen, surprised to find a notification from the Jinx app. I'd almost given up on the dating app giving me any matches. Perhaps I was too picky. But what was a witch to do? It wasn't like I could just ignore my standards.

Kuk matched with you.

I clicked on the profile, surprised to find an

attractive man with a kind smile and eyes that seemed as if they were lost in thought. Despite knowing that it probably wouldn't lead anywhere, I opened the chat.

< Hey. > I paused before hitting send, realising that I should probably say something *more*, but I couldn't find the words to. I was always rubbish at starting conversations with attractive men on the app, or in person if I was honest. No matter how many lists I read, or how much I asked my friends for help, I couldn't seem to crack the formula for good openings.

Hopefully, Kuk would be better at it than I was because once I got going, I'd be fine. The problem was getting there and I had to wonder how many connections I missed as a result.

I glanced over to where Baal and Chelsea were doing their normal back-and-forth. She touched his arm, he leaned in closer and murmured something to her, making her blush. One of these days, the two of them were going to have to go on a date and finally explore whatever it was between them. If they didn't, then I was going to be really disappointed. Which definitely suggested that I was more invested in their relationship than I should be, even if Chelsea was my friend.

In short, it was definitely time to find something

to occupy my time with that wasn't about pushing one of my friends into the arms of someone she clearly wanted.

I hit send before I could chicken out.

I took a deep breath and set my phone down to try and focus on something other than checking it every thirty seconds to see if he'd responded already.

I wiped down the side and had almost managed to stop thinking about it when my screen lit up.

I checked that the other two weren't paying any attention and grabbed my phone.

< Hello, Anise. > For reasons completely unknown to me, I read the words in a deep voice that resonated within me along with a sense of excitement about the possibility of this match. It didn't feel the same as when I'd matched with other men, but I couldn't put my finger on what it was.

We exchanged a few boring pleasantries, but even that didn't do anything to dispel the feeling.

Chelsea's surprisingly loud laugh startled me and I looked up only to find her leaning over and showing something to Baal. I resisted the urge to roll my eyes. They were so into each other.

A message lit up my screen and I pulled it up, my heart sinking as I read the message.

< You're a witch, aren't you? >

I swallowed hard and thought of the right way to respond. There was a chance Kuk was paranormal too, but there was no way of being sure of that, and one wrong move could mean that I accidentally exposed myself in a way I wasn't supposed to.

I typed back with shaky fingers. < Haha, is that cause I put you under a spell? > I hit send and tried not to worry about any repercussions.

< It was a genuine question. >

I stared at his response, trying to think of the right way to deal with it, but before I could come up with one, another message popped up.

< I'm sorry, I shouldn't have asked. It's just that I recognised the charm you were wearing in your fourth photo and I haven't seen it in a long time. >

I let out a sigh of relief, but still clicked through to my photos to check what he was talking about. Sure enough, the fourth photo was one of me at my sister's wedding wearing a witch-charm that was supposed to bring good luck to the happy couple.

I clicked back onto the chat and thought through a few possible responses before settling on one.

< So if I'm a witch, what are you? >

< You wouldn't believe me if I told you. > The response came quickly, sending a small thrill through me as I realised he was waiting for me to respond.

Hopefully, there wouldn't be a new customer arriving soon who needed my attention.

< Try me. I don't spook easily. > What was he likely to be? If he was worried about my reaction, then maybe he was a vampire. Or a fae. They didn't have the best reputation these days.

< I'm a god. >

I squeaked and dropped my phone. It clattered against the service desk, drawing a concerned look from Chelsea.

"I'm fine," I said quickly, though I could hear that I wasn't.

She didn't look convinced.

"I'm good," I said firmly.

"If you're sure?" Concern was written all over her face, but I waved her away. Even if I was actually dealing with something, I wouldn't want to take her away from Baal. Not if it could result in her actually finally getting a date with him.

< A god? > I typed back, wondering if this was real, or if it was all part of an elaborate prank. < You're not going to follow that up by saying you're a god in bed, are you? >

< I'm a god everywhere. >

I snorted. < I can't tell if you're being serious, or if this is an elaborate chat up line. > Except that wasn't true. Something within me was screaming that he was telling the truth, and that this wasn't just a ploy.

< I'm just a man in bed. >

Bemusement filled me. < Easy to please, but ultimately disappointing? >

< Maybe I'm a god there after all. >

< Is this where you say there's only one way for me to find out? > I hit send before I had a chance to think about it.

The return bubble popped up within seconds, making it clear that he was as invested in this conversation as I was. Then again, I supposed that wasn't too surprising considering what we were talking about.

< I'd only say something like that after we'd been on a few dates. >

I raised an eyebrow. Either he was really good at playing the game he needed to, or he was being sincere.

< Let's chat a bit more before we agree to that. > The message felt risky. But then again, if sex was the only thing he was after, then scaring him off wasn't a big deal. I was past looking for a night of

entertainment and was ready to find something more.

And for the first time in months, I was starting to feel as if I might find that on Jinx.

TWO

Anise

I STEPPED out of the shower and wrapped my towel closely around my body, a small shiver running through me as the cool air hit my skin. This was always the worst part.

I grabbed my phone from where I'd left it on the bathroom counter so I could shut off the shower playlist I had going. There were certain songs that I only liked to listen to while I was washing, which I realised was a bit strange, but I saw no reason to deprive myself of my shower jams because of it. I hit the pause button and dismissed the app. A notification from Jinx caught my eye from where it was waiting at the top of the screen and my heart skipped a beat in response. I knew who it was going to be. It had been a week since I'd stopped using the app to find other people. There wasn't any point when just a simple conversation with Kuk was enough to make me certain I wasn't going to find anyone else I wanted to talk to.

The god was going to ruin me for everyone else, I could sense it. And yet there was a part of me that was eager for that to happen.

I opened the message, smiling to see that it was just him asking how I was.

< Sorry, not ignoring you, I was in the shower. > I hit send, knowing that my message was going to make him think about me naked. It was cheeky, but it was the right tone for the way our conversation was going. The flirting had been coming thick and fast, so it felt like the right time to make things a little more suggestive. And just the idea of the sexy god on the other end of the conversation thinking about me naked was enough to set my body on fire.

< That's okay, I was too. > His reply came quickly, reassuring me that he wasn't annoyed by my delayed reply. Not that I'd really expected him to be.

< Nope, don't believe that's possible. You're just trying to make me think about you shirtless. > I bit my lip as I sent the response. It was certainly a little more risqué than any of the messages I'd sent to the other matches I'd made on Jinx, but something about the way Kuk talked to me made me feel safe.

< Why think? >

A photo flashed up under the message and my mouth went dry. His broad chest was covered in small water droplets, only making it seem that much hotter, and his waist was wrapped in a towel, leaving no doubt in my mind that he was telling the truth.

Somehow my own attempt at making him think about me that way had backfired and resulted in me getting all hot and flustered myself.

I glanced at my reflection in the mirror and realised that my cheeks were slightly flushed just from the thought of it all.

I bit my lip and considered how I should be responding. It wasn't like me to be this way, but something about him was making me bold. I turned on my camera and rearranged my towel a bit so it looked a bit more suggestive than it actually was. I was definitely guilty of picking my towels based on comfort and not on the chances for sex appeal.

I took the photo and checked that it looked the way I wanted to, making sure to cut off my face. I wasn't an idiot. Even if I felt like I could trust Kuk, and the photo wasn't even that explicit, this was still the internet.

< I can send proof too. > I attached the image and hit send, hoping he wasn't going to find it too forward.

But that wasn't likely. I might have started the shower conversation, but he was the one who sent the first photo, this was all on him.

< I might need to get back in and turn the water as cold as it goes. >

I chuckled. < Isn't that what you do when you want to stop being hot and bothered? >

< It is. >

< Then I don't see why you'd want a cold shower. > I certainly didn't. No matter how far away he was, I liked the idea of him thinking about me like this.

< If I didn't know better, I'd say you were being a tease, Anise. >

< You're the one who sent me a photo of your bare chest. >

< Like what you see? >

I chewed on my bottom lip. < Almost as much as

if you'd been in the shower with me. > A small thrill went through me as I hit send.

I hoped that he was as affected by the conversation as me.

I made my way back to my bedroom and flopped down on the bed. There was a lot of truth in my words. I would very much like it if he was here with me, but I knew that it was probably too soon for that.

Maybe.

< If I was there, maybe we'd still be in the shower. >

< Or maybe you'd have come to join me on my bed. > I hit send without thinking about it, but I didn't care. Something about messaging Kuk was so easy. Despite being on the other end of the phone, he was making me comfortable in a way no one had in a very long time.

< Is that an invitation, Anise? >

< Maybe a future one. But I think we'd need to go on a proper date first. > My whole body tingled at the thought. It was going to be hard to stick to my resolve, so it would have to be a date somewhere public.

< I wouldn't dream of it any other way. > His response was instant and only added to the way I was feeling about the whole situation.

Another message popped up before I could respond. < So, what kind of date do you like the best? >

< I don't really have a favourite. It all depends on the company. > My fingers almost fumbled over the keyboard as I typed. < I think I'd enjoy any date with you. >

< Ah, so my challenge is to make the date as terrible as possible just to check if it was what you really wanted? >

I snorted. < That's mean. A nice date would still be preferred. >

< I will keep that in mind when we get a chance to go on one. >

< Will that be soon? > I hoped it was going to be. Normally, I'd want to keep talking to him via Jinx for a lot longer, but there was almost a sense of urgency within me whenever I thought about meeting him in person. It was a need unlike any I'd ever experienced before. Maybe I was imagining it, but I could feel as if this was the start of something big. Whether it turned into anything serious or not, I was never going to be able to forget matching with Kuk, I was certain of it.

< I'd like it if it was. >

Relief filled me as I read his response. That was a good thing. I wanted him to feel the same way I did, and everything he was saying suggested that he did.

Excitement for the future filled me. I had no idea what was going to happen, but I could tell that it was going to be good.

THREE

Jinx

KUK

I LOOKED out of the window, unsurprised to find darkness was falling. I could sense it within me, which made perfect sense considering what I was the god of. My sister might technically be the one linked to dusk, but our magic was so tightly entwined that it was hard to tell where mine stopped and hers started. Luckily, our lives were much more separate.

Another day was over, and another night was beginning, just like it had happened for thousands of years. And just like it will be for thousands of years to come. There were very few things that stayed the same in the world, but this was one of them.

My phone lit up from its spot on my desk and I found an involuntary smile spreading over my face.

I guessed that some things did change. I picked it up and opened the Jinx app without even considering that it could be another notification. That wasn't going to be the case. I could feel deep within me that it was Anise. I didn't know what it was about her, but despite never having seen her in person, I felt a deep connection to her unlike I had to anyone else. She was special, every part of me screamed that was the truth.

I opened our chat to find a photo waiting for me, bringing a smile to my face even if it wasn't as risqué as the ones she'd been sending. Not that I could talk. I'd been appreciating every pixel and hoping she felt the same about the photos I sent her in return.

I sucked in a deep breath as I took in the bountiful dark curls which framed her face, making her look more seductive than anyone had a right to with her parted lips and knowing glint in her eyes. It was the dress that really did me in though, especially with the clearly purposeful hint of cleavage she'd sent. She was gorgeous in a way I couldn't describe with words.

Something stirred within me, and I didn't think it was all to do with how she looked physically either.

< You look beautiful. > I hit send, not even worrying about how she was going to respond.

< I was hoping for hot. >

A smirk lifted the side of my lips. She was definitely that. < I was going for the gentlemanly answer. >

< I think we might be past that. >

Yes, we probably were. I couldn't remember the last time I'd been so consumed with the need to talk to someone, but every time a message from Anise popped up, I felt like I had to respond to her, and that it was important for us to talk. She was special, even if I wasn't entirely sure how.

< Then you look incredibly hot. > I sent back.

< Better. >

< So, where are you going? > And what was the chance that I was going to be able to get there? That made me sound more possessive than I was, but it wasn't about that. I didn't care how many people looked at her, or how many wanted her. It was all about the fact that *I* wanted her.

< We're going to a speed dating event downtown. >

My whole world stopped. Why would she be

going somewhere like that? I thought things were going well here. < Speed dating? >

< Yes, are you going? >

< Why would I be going? >

< There are supposed to be gods who go to this one. I was kind of hoping you'd be there. >

I blinked a few times, knowing exactly what event she was talking about. She was right, there would be *lots* of gods in attendance. My sister went there a lot and from what she said, it was going to be packed with the hottest gods and paranormals around.

The thought of the gorgeous witch I'd been chatting to via the Jinx app sitting opposite charming gods from all over the world, flirting and potentially even liking them, had jealousy rising up within me to an extent that I hadn't felt in years. This wasn't normal for me.

A reckless and unfair thought that I could persuade Kuaket to go and keep an eye on her crossed my mind. But I wasn't that kind of person.

If I didn't want to think about her flirting with other gods, then the simple solution was to go myself.

A message popped up on the screen.

< Will you be there? >

My heart started to race. Maybe I wasn't the

only one who was thinking about the situation in this way.

< I have no need for speed dating. >

< But you do of a dating app? > Despite the fact the message was sent via the app, I could hear the teasing note in her words.

< I had the need before I met you. >

< Is it really meeting if we've only ever talked via Jinx? >

I let out a shaky breath. There was an invitation in her words if I ever heard one. Now all I had to do was take the plunge and act on it.

< Maybe it's time we change that. > I hit send before I could think twice about it.

< What did you have in mind? > Her messages were coming through so fast that I had to assume she was waiting for them, something that gave me hope that I wouldn't have to sit at home thinking about her sitting opposite all the gods I'd ever met.

< That depends. Do you want a drink? Dinner? > My fingers almost tripped over themselves as I typed.

< Drinks sound good. Twenty minutes? > Anise's response was almost instant.

< You want to meet tonight? >

< Unless you have someone else to go out with. >

< There is no one else I'm interested in. > No one

had caught my interest like Anise had in the short space of time I'd been talking to her. Not in several decades.

< Have you been to the Rose Hip Bar? >

< No. Where is it? > I'd check, but that would mean clicking away from our chat.

< Downtown. I'll see you there in an hour? >

One hour. That was all it was going to be until I got to put a proper face to the name and words that made up Anise in my head. I couldn't wait.

< Won't you miss your speed dating event? > I didn't want her to go to it, but I also didn't want her to end up regretting that.

< There was only one god I was going there to see. >

< Zeus, right? >

I hoped she laughed. I imagined that she did.

< Absolutely. It's him I'm planning on ditching my friends for. >

< I hope he's worth it. >

< I'm certain he will be. >

A warm feeling spread through me at her words. I was confident that this was going to go well. I couldn't explain exactly what it was between us, or how I could tell that it was something special over a messaging app, but there was no denying the way she made me feel.

My phone screen lit up again. < I'm looking forward to meeting you properly, Kuk. >

< Likewise. > I dropped my phone onto the sofa and headed to the bathroom. If I needed to be at the Rose Hip Bar in an hour, then I needed to shower and get dressed as quickly as I could. I didn't want to keep her waiting when this was my chance to make a good impression.

Should I get her some flowers? No, there wasn't time for that. I was just going to have to hope that I was enough. And I could always send her some tomorrow.

Excitement rose within me as I realised that this was it. I was going to meet the woman who had been occupying most of my thoughts for the past few weeks.

It was a good thing that I didn't have to wait.

FOUR

ANISE

I ENTERED the Rose Hip Bar and waited for a sense of nervousness to overcome me. But it didn't. This all felt right.

Even more so when my gaze landed on the handsome man waiting by the bar.

Kuk.

I had absolutely no doubt that it was him. It wasn't even that he looked like his photo, it was just something about the whole aura he was giving off. I could sense that this was the man I was interested in.

He looked up at the door as I walked in, a wide

smile crossing his face, making me certain he'd recognised me in much the same way as I had him.

My heart skipped a beat, and a delicious kind of nervousness I wasn't used to sprang to life inside me. This moment was going to be an important one, even if I couldn't exactly define why in words.

I headed over to the bar, relishing the way he watched me cross over to him. There was no doubt that he was just as pleased by my appearance as I was by his. Which reassured me that my impromptu suggestion to meet up wasn't unfounded. I didn't feel so guilty about abandoning Chelsea and Delia to their fate at speed dating. They'd be fine, especially as I'd spied Baal before I left. Hopefully, Chelsea would finally get the chance to make a connection with him outside the Copy Shop.

All of those thoughts fled from my mind as I got to the bar.

Kuk straightened as I approached. "Hello, Anise," he said in a low voice that sent a pleasant shiver down my spine.

"Hi." It came out breathlessly, which was partly due to the intensity with which he was looking at me.

He flagged down the bartender and flashed me a smile. "What would you like to drink?"

"A mojito," I said, taking the opportunity to rake

my gaze up and down him. Everything about him screamed power, but in an effortless way that I knew wasn't going to hurt me.

He nodded. "Make that two."

"You don't have to drink the same thing as me."

"I know, but I actually like them," he assured me. "I picked up a taste for them on a beach in South America a few years ago."

"Out of interest, when you say a few years, do you mean one or two, or a decade?" I'd avoided asking any questions about his status as a god up until now, but it was impossible to ignore the opportunity.

He chuckled. "I don't actually know the answer to that."

The bartender set two drinks in front of us and Kuk handed over his card for a tab.

"Do you want to stay here or do you want to grab a seat?" he asked.

"I like the look of the corner booth," I responded.

He raised an eyebrow.

I reached out for my drink, purposefully brushing against him as I did.

He cleared his throat. "The booth it is."

I headed over in that direction, aware of his gaze boring into me as I walked away. With every step, I felt more powerful and desirable than ever, despite being in the presence of an actual god.

I slipped into the booth, trying not to think about how much the skirt of my dress rode up as I did. Or maybe I shouldn't care.

No. I was here on a date. This was about more than just the physical connection between us, it was about the way he made me feel when we talked. Though there was no denying how hot he was.

But I supposed that wasn't news to me. I'd seen photos of what was under his shirt.

Kuk sat down beside me, shuffling in, but not sitting close enough that we were touching. That was fine. I imagined that we'd end up changing that before too long.

I ran my fingers up and down the stem of my glass without thinking.

"I'm sorry you're missing your speed dating event," he said.

"I'm not. I was mostly going because my friend needed a distraction from this guy she's been pining over. Though I thought I saw him before I left."

"I've heard a lot of people go," he responded.

"You know of it?"

He nodded. "My sister goes a lot. Mostly when she wants to hook up with someone."

"Ah, so no using dating apps like you, then?" I

asked, curious about what had made him decide to use it in the first place when he could clearly go out to any bar in the city and pick someone up without much effort.

"Kua and I are very different people."

"Even if you're gods of the same thing?" I asked. "Sorry, I should have admitted to researching you."

He chuckled. "I think it's reasonable for you to have done that as soon as I told you I was a god."

"I waited until I got home from work at least," I responded.

"Did you like what you found?"

"I like what you've told me more." I picked up my glass and took a sip, enjoying the minty freshness of the mojito. "The internet told me what you are, but it didn't tell me anything about you. Lucky for me, you did a good job of that." I brushed my hand against his arm.

"I'm glad you feel that way."

"I wouldn't be here if I didn't," I responded. "I don't waste my time on connections that I don't think are real."

"I don't either," he responded, leaning closer.

Every time he moved, I gained a new awareness of his body. Heat rolled off him in waves, though I suspected that some of it was the way he was making me feel.

I cleared my throat and tried to focus on my drink, but I wasn't able to keep my mind off the handsome man beside me. Then again, I supposed we'd agreed to meet with the knowledge that this was a date, and that made things different.

"I don't even know what I'm supposed to ask you," I say. "What do people talk about on dates?"

He raised an eyebrow. "Haven't you been going on any?"

"Yes. But they weren't like this," I admitted. "We'd start with small talk and I'd end up laughing awkwardly, that kind of thing. This is different."

"Different how?" An intrigued expression crossed his face as he leaned closer.

"I don't know. I can't explain it. It just feels as if this is *more*. Do you know what I mean?" It was nerve-wracking to put the way I was feeling out in the open, especially when we hadn't spent much time together in person yet. But there was no getting around the fact that we'd spent weeks going back and forth chatting and talking to one another.

This was more than just a fleeting connection, and I was sure of it.

He turned to me, his eyes glittering with the same emotions that were going through me. "It is more."

I bit my lip and his gaze instantly dropped there.

28

Something curled up inside me, building into the desire to move this to the next phase.

Kuk seemed to feel the same, as he reached out and brushed his fingers against my cheek.

My breathing hitched and all rational thoughts disappeared as I considered what was coming. I didn't need to ask to be certain of his intentions, I could see it written on his face.

He paused for a moment, presumably to give me a chance to get out of the current situation if I wanted to.

But I didn't.

I moved closer, getting caught in the heavy anticipation lingering in the air. It was almost like a physical presence as it built, the tempting scent of the god beside me only serving to make me want this more.

I came here knowing how this was likely to end, and now that was within my grasp, I was even more certain it was what I wanted.

My eyes fluttered closed just as Kuk's lips brushed against mine. His lips tasted of the mint and lime from the mojito, but that was only a fleeting thought before I became caught up in the moment. His free hand rested on my waist, and I could feel the heat of his palm through the fabric of my dress, making me wish that it wasn't between us.

I deepened the kiss, trying not to imagine how this would feel if we were completely alone, and how much better that would be. How we wouldn't have to stop and could just follow where our instincts took us.

Because one thing was abundantly clear to me with this kiss. It wasn't enough. I needed more of him, and I wasn't going to be satisfied unless I could get it.

The kiss ended, but we didn't pull away from one another. He was so close that his breath tickled my lips, making it impossible for me not to think of what had just been, and what was to come.

"That was better than I imagined," he murmured.

"Was I a bad kisser in your imagination?"

He chuckled, the sound vibrating through me thanks to our proximity. "Far from it. But the reality is still so much better."

"I know what you mean." I bit my lip, considering whether I wanted to suggest what was on my mind. "Do you want to get out of here?"

"Are you hungry?"

"Not for food."

Surprise flashed over his face, followed by a deepening desire.

"Come back to mine," I whispered. I hadn't

thought through the words, but the moment I said them out loud, I knew they were what I wanted.

"Are you sure?"

"I've never been more sure of anything," I admitted.

For a moment, I thought he was going to say no, but then he nodded.

Excitement flooded through me. I couldn't explain why I was so certain about him, but I was.

This was the right decision, I could feel it in every part of me, and I knew that this was going to be the start of something, even if I didn't know precisely how it was going to go.

FIVE

ANISE

FLUTTERS FILLED my stomach as I slipped my key into the lock and twisted it, opening the door to my flat. I knew I was the one who had suggested this, but it didn't quite negate the way I was feeling. Though it was hard to put a finger on whether it was actually nerves, or if it was excitement.

Kuk reached out and placed a hand on my lower back, and from the firmness of his touch, I realised I knew the answer after all.

It was *definitely* excitement.

He paused at the threshold, not taking the final step inside.

"Is everything okay?" I asked, worry filling me. Had I made him uncomfortable suggesting this? Should I have waited for a few more dates first? I pushed the thought aside. After our kiss in the bar, there was no ignoring whatever it was brewing between us.

"Are you sure you want me to come in?" He brushed his hand against my back as he asked, sending a bolt of desire through me, which I doubted was his intention, but it was an undeniable result regardless of that.

"Yes." My answer was instant. I wanted this.

I reached out to take his hand in mine and stepped over the threshold into my flat, pulling him along with me.

He shut the door behind us, and I was more grateful than ever for the automatic locking system that it was set up with, it meant that I didn't have to waste a moment in leading him to my bedroom.

Something seemed to unleash inside him as we stepped inside and he pulled me to him. I wrapped my arms around his neck and wasted no time in pressing my lips against his.

This kiss was hungrier than the one in the bar, and I could feel the desire rising inside me just at the feel of his whole body against mine, even if we were still fully dressed.

I trailed my hand down until my fingers were playing with the buttons of his shirt. I hesitated for a moment, knowing that there was no going back once I started undoing them.

Kuk broke the kiss and looked at me with concern in his eyes. "Are you okay?"

"Yes, sorry." My voice cracked as I spoke.

"We don't have to do anything you don't want."

"I know. And the same goes for you. I don't want to rush you into anything you don't want either."

"I'm not being rushed," he promised. "But if you are..."

"I'm not," I cut him off, not wanting him to think for a moment that was looking at him in a bad light. "But I'm not used to feeling like this."

He nodded. "I can understand that. So why don't we take sex off the table."

I let out a small disappointed sigh without meaning to.

A satisfied smirk twisted at the corners of Kuk's lips. "I didn't say *everything* had to be off the table."

"Or we can just go with what feels right?" I suggested instead.

"Only if you promise that you'll tell me if you want to stop."

"I will."

"Good," he murmured, his breath tickling my lips.

I leaned in and kissed him deeply, starting to unbutton his shirt as I did. All of the hesitation from before drifted away and was replaced by a quiet confidence that I knew wasn't going anywhere. It's surreal what even a small conversation about what the two of us both need can do, but there's no doubt it's put my mind at ease.

His fingers grazed my leg where my dress ended, and a shot of desire flew through me in response. There was going to be no stopping us once we started, and that was just fine by me.

I had to break the kiss in order to push his shirt off his shoulders, and he took the opportunity to draw my dress over my head, leaving me standing in my bra and panties. Kuk's gaze raked over me, the desire in his eyes making me feel as if I was the most beautiful woman in the world.

I could get used to this.

I bit my lip and made my way over to the bed, drawing him closer with a gentle touch on his arm. I leaned back on the covers, and he followed me, caging me in with his arms but not making me feel trapped. All I had to do was say the word, and he'd let me get up. I just didn't want that.

He kissed me, his body pressing against mine.

The touch of his hand against my bare leg was almost too much for me, and I let out a small moan.

He broke away from my lips and began to kiss my neck. I squirmed beneath the touch, anticipation building within me as he did. I arched my back and he slipped his hand underneath to unclasp my bra, pulling it off and throwing it to the side. The cool air hit my nipples, making the sensations even more acute when Kuk reached them and took one in his mouth.

I let out a low moan, unable to help myself. This was almost too much. He moved further down, leaving a trail of heat after him as he kissed across my stomach, and further down.

A soft squeak escaped from me without me realising that was the noise I was going to make. He hooked his fingers under the band of my panties and pulled them down, baring me to him.

He looked up and met my gaze, and I could sense him searching for any hint that I was uncomfortable, which only served to turn me on more. I didn't think I'd ever considered that someone being so attentive, not just to my physical needs but to my emotional ones too, could make me feel this way, but there was no doubt that was what was happening. He was worshipping me, there was no other way of putting it.

He kissed the inside of my thigh, each touch only sending me closer towards the edge. I parted my legs more, but he seemed too intent on his task to notice.

The moment he reached my centre, my eyes rolled back and I gripped the sheets with my left hand. He took that for confirmation he was doing the right thing and repeated the same motion again. Desire built up within me, and it was everything I could do to hold back the release that was building. Letting go wouldn't be the end of this, but I still wanted to prolong the sensations for as long as possible.

"Kuk," I murmured as it all became too much. Though his name was more of a plea than anything else, something he seemed to realise.

I tipped over the edge, my entire body beginning to shake and a loud groan escaping from me as my mind emptied and my release took over.

I lost track of everything as it fades away and I slump back onto the bed. "Wow."

Kuk chuckles. "I didn't expect that to happen so fast."

"You shouldn't laugh at that, you might be even faster," I murmured.

"That's true."

"But you're very dressed still."

A knowing smirk crossed his face as he got to his feet and stripped off the rest of his clothing, leaving him gloriously naked in front of me. Just as I'd suspected, it was even better to have him in front of me than it had been to have seen photos of his bare chest.

"Condom," I blurted, turning over so I could reach into my bedside drawer.

Kuk let out a groan from behind me, and I realised I hadn't thought about the fact that I was just as naked as he was. Something about his presence was putting me so at ease that it barely mattered.

Other than the fact he was enjoying the view.

I located one of the foil packets I was looking for, moving with exaggerated slowness now that I knew he was enjoying the show. There was no reason not to prolong it as much as I could when we were both having fun.

"You're going to be the death of me," he said as I turned around.

"Is that so?"

"Mmhm."

I dropped the condom onto the bed and went up on my knees so our faces were on the same level. I leaned in and kissed him deeply. There was no doubt that there was a physical attraction between us, but despite the fact that we were naked right now, it was clear that there was more to it too.

I leaned back, drawing him onto the bed and over me. I broke the kiss but only so I could find where the condom had fallen. I opened it quickly and slipped my hands between us so I could put it on him. He groaned at my touch, desire clouding his eyes as he looked at me.

The feeling in the air intensified as we guided ourselves into position, and the moment he entered me, I became more convinced than ever about how serious this was.

I lost myself in the way it felt to have his body moving with mine, and the intensity of the connection it was producing. This didn't feel like an *end-of-date-one* kind of night, which made me certain that the decision to invite him here was a good one.

There was no going back now that my heart was under the spell of a god.

SIX

KUK

THE DOOR to my office swung open and I looked up, vaguely annoyed to discover that it was my sister walking into my office and not Anise, even though I knew it wasn't possible for her to. She had work and didn't actually know where my office was. Two things that would make it hard for her to visit me here.

"What can I do for you, Kua?" I asked.

"Is that any way to greet me, brother?" She dropped down into the visitor's chair on the other side of my desk and threw her legs over the arm without a single care for how she should be properly sitting on it.

I rolled my eyes. "You never come here unless you want something."

"Maybe I was just passing and wanted a chat."

"Mmhmm." I set down my pen and studied her intently. "Guy problems?"

"Pfft, please. You know I don't have those."

"If you're still dating that warlock, then we know you have them." I took a sip of water, but mostly to stop myself from berating her over her choice again. I knew there was nothing I could say that would change her mind about the man, even if I thought it was going to end in disaster.

"We're not dating, Kuk. Don't be so old-fashioned. You can sleep with someone without being in love with them, you know."

I choked on the water.

Kua raised an eyebrow, a knowing smile spreading over her face. "You slept with someone."

Memories of the night before assailed me. Not that the thought of Anise falling apart in my arms was something that was ever really far from my thoughts today.

"Ah, but you love them already." The way she said it made it sound as if she was disappointed in me.

"I don't." Yet.

"But it wasn't just a one-night stand, was it?"

"No." At least, I certainly hoped it wasn't. My gut told me that I was right about that.

"Oh, Kuk, what am I going to do with you?"

"Just tell me why you're here, Kua." I tried to keep the exasperation out of my voice, but I didn't think I managed very well.

She sighed. "Fine. Did you hear from Horus recently?"

"About the calendar he's having Baal shoot for him?"

"Ah, so you did."

"It would be hard to forget an invitation to take part in a naked calendar of gods," I pointed out.

"Are you doing it?"

"No." I couldn't think of anything worse, though I was confident that between Horus and Baal, they'd be able to find more than enough people willing to take part in their project.

"Aww, don't be a spoilsport. Don't you want to help the kids? Or the cats. Or whatever it is the charity supports."

"It's for Horus' animal sanctuary." Which would know if she'd read the email properly.

"Ah." She shrugged. "It sounds fun. I'm doing it."

"Of course you are." I shook my head in bemusement.

"You should try getting out of your shell a bit more, you might like it there," she said.

"I'm a few thousand years old, I'm not about to change everything about myself now."

"Suit yourself." She got to her feet.

I raised an eyebrow. "That's it?"

"I told you, I was in the area, so I dropped in to see you. There was nothing nefarious about my intentions."

"Which is unusual," I muttered.

"You wound me, brother." She smiled and headed out to the door. "I look forward to meeting the person you're seeing."

I resisted the urge to tell her that that would never happen, partly because I knew it would if I kept seeing Anise. Kuaket was the person who had known me for the longest, anyone who was a big part of my life would have to meet her.

My phone lit up, and I grabbed it without thinking, smiling at the notification from the Jinx app.

< Work is extra boring when I know I could still be in bed with you. >

I chuckled. < For me too. >

< It's a shame we couldn't call in sick and just hang out there all day. >

< When's your next day off? > I hoped she was going to say soon because the idea of having to go another week *without* being able to spend a whole day in bed with her would be torture.

< Wednesday. >

< Then we should make plans. > It was only after I hit send that I realised she might not want to. < That is if you want to go on a second date. >

< I was planning on it. I might already be thinking about our third date. >

< What were you planning? > I was grinning like a fool while messaging her, which wasn't actually anything new. She'd been having this effect on me the entire time, it was just even more pronounced now that I knew what it was like to fall asleep next to her.

There was no way I'd be able to forget Anise now.

< Nothing that involves being around other people. >

< You're insatiable. > Not that I was complaining.

< Only with you. But you're a god, you can keep up. >

< You know it. > I leaned back in my chair and let out a contented smile. I wasn't sure precisely what made me download the Jinx app in the first place. I supposed I was feeling lonely, especially with a lot of my friends starting to go to speed dating events and meeting people there. But that wasn't for me. There were entirely too many people at those kinds of events, and I didn't want to put myself through that.

But even so, I never expected to find someone like Anise on the app. A real connection that I felt could go somewhere. I hadn't even had the hint of that in a long time.

And I wasn't going to waste a moment of it. I went back to our chat and typed out the message I really wanted to send. < Are you free tonight? >

< Yes. >

I let out a sigh of relief. If she was responding that fast, it meant that she was thinking about this just as much as I was.

< How about dinner at mine? >

< Are you cooking for me, Kuk? >

< Don't you mean *kuking*? > I was glad I knew what her laughter sounded like now, it meant that I could hear it in my head, even if the joke was terrible.

< How long have you been waiting to use that one? >

I took a sip of my water before responding. < Longer than I want to admit. My sister says it's a terrible joke and if I tell it to people, they won't want to date me. >

< Well, I think it's cute and your sister is wrong. >

She didn't know the half of what was wrong with the things Kua said, but I wasn't about to dive down that path. I was sure Anise would discover Kua's eccentricities in time.

< In which case, I'll be making the most elaborate feast you can imagine. > Though I had no idea how I was going to do that. I wasn't a bad cook, but elaborate might be a stretch.

< Make sure you leave room for dessert. >

< Is dessert you? > I hit send without thinking about it, but that was okay. Clearly we had a good measure of one another.

< My plan was a chocolate cake from the bakery down the road, but I'm more than happy to change the menu. >

< Both sounds good. > Despite saying that, I had no doubt which of the two would be occupying my mind for the rest of the day.

< Both it is. >

I was grinning from ear to ear when I set the phone down. I hoped no one needed anything from me for the rest of the day, because I wasn't convinced that I was going to be any use for anyone at work. Not when my head was full of an enchanting witch who I couldn't wait to see again.

SEVEN

Jinx

ANISE

I WASN'T sure what I expected from the home of a god, but it wasn't the fancy building that I'd found myself in. It made me wonder why Kuk wanted to see me again after being to my tiny flat.

I rang the doorbell and shifted the box with the chocolate cake in my arm so it didn't fall.

What was I doing here? He was clearly so out of my league that it was unthinkable that I could do this.

The door swung open, and all of my doubts fled from my mind as I took in Kuk's handsome form standing in the doorway. He smiled widely, his whole face lighting up as he took me in.

"Hey," I said.

"Hi." He leaned in to kiss my cheek, knocking the box off balance in the process.

He reached out to grab it.

"Let me." I raised my other hand and sent a bolt of magic in the direction of the box, steadying it without any need for either of our hands. "I should have thought to carry it with magic before."

"There are humans around outside," he reminded me.

"Yeah, but they'd just think I was using invisible strings, it's been a long time since they jumped to *magic* as an explanation."

"Has it?"

"Your age is showing," I teased, going up my toes and kissing his cheek.

"Is that weird for you?" he asked as he stepped aside to let me into the flat.

Unsurprisingly, it was just as beautiful inside as the building was outside, with a lot of monochrome furniture in a style that suited him. The only thing that was out of place was a huge antique bookcase that looked to be filled with things he'd collected over the years. I hoped to get a chance to hear him talk about them in the future.

"Your age?" I checked.

He nodded and took the cake from me, releasing my magic in the process.

I shrugged. "I can't say I've really thought about it. I've dated vampires before, and known other people who did. And witches don't age normally anyway. It's just a number, unless you're about to tell me you're going to lock me in a nunnery or something."

"Absolutely not."

"Then no, it's not an issue." I took off my coat and he took it from me, his fingers brushing against the bare skin of my arm as he does.

"I'm glad." He takes it away and comes back with a glass of wine.

"You're not even going to ask if I want red or white?"

He chuckled. "I got the wine you said you liked."

"Kuk! That's fifty quid for a bottle."

"You said you liked it. And that's not exactly an issue."

I narrowed my eyes at him. "What exactly do you do for work?"

"You mean other than having spent several thousand years amassing wealth?" he joked.

"I imagine that helps." I took the glass from him and took a small sip of the wine, enjoying the taste even if I knew that it was an expensive vintage. It was sweet of him to get it, even if it was pricey.

"It does," he agreed. "But I'm actually a property lawyer."

"That's not what I expected."

"Why not?"

"I don't know, you're the god of darkness, shouldn't you be..." I trailed off. "I actually have no idea what would be the perfect job for your godliness."

"Something at night, I guess?" Amusement danced through his eyes.

"Yeah, I realised that was a dumb thing to say."

"Not dumb at all. If it helps, Bastet runs a cat sanctuary."

"It *does* help," I assured him. "That's much more in line with what I expected."

"And Menhit makes custom knives."

"I don't know what he's the god of," I admitted, not recognising the name.

"She's a war goddess. Let's see, who else has jobs that match their domain. Seth's an architect, so I'm not sure that counts."

"I'm not sure I'd want to be living in a building designed by the god of chaos," I muttered.

"You'd be surprised, he's always pointing out that without chaos there can't be order," Kuk said.

"Oh, Horus runs an animal sanctuary, but it started life as just a bird of prey sanctuary. Does that one satisfy your need for the right job for the right god?"

"It does, thank you." I followed him into the large open-plan kitchen. "So what made you become a property lawyer?"

"The fact I wouldn't have to deal with many people," he admitted. "I'm not very sociable. We'd never have met at your speed dating event."

"Then it's a good thing that you decided to download Jinx."

"A *very* good thing." He gave me a look that said just how much he thought that. "You said you were still going to night school?"

I nodded. "I needed to get out of a bad situation and ended up dropping out of university when I was nineteen. It's been ten years, but I'm finally working on finishing my programming qualifications."

"An interesting choice for a witch," he teased.

"Not when you learn that this witch has aspirations of starting an app for working out your potion shopping. Basically, it'll be like going on one of the supermarket apps, but for potions instead of food."

"I can see a market for that."

"Though maybe what we really need is a dating app that's just for paranormals and gods. Why doesn't that exist yet?" I asked offhandedly. I would have gone for that instead of Jinx if it had been an option.

He shrugged. "Isn't that what Jinx is?"

I frowned. "Huh, I hadn't thought about it, but you're right. I only ever saw paranormals on there. I wonder ifthey're in need of a programmer who understands both code and magic."

The way he looked at me made me feel as if he thought the idea was a great one, and it made me glow with pride. I didn't need his approval in order to work on something like this, but it always meant a lot when someone thought my ideas were good.

"I can find out who to ask," he said.

"You don't need to do that."

"But I want to." He flashed me a reassuring smile that made me certain of the truth in his words.

I took another sip of wine. "This is really good."

"It is," he agreed. "I can see why you like it. I'll have to get more of it."

"You really don't have to."

"Then what am I supposed to do with my amassed riches?" From the twinkle in his eye, I had to assume he was teasing.

"You weren't joking about those, were you?" I asked.

Kuk chuckled. "Sort of. It's not as much as some

of the other gods have managed, and I still need to work. But it's certainly enough that I can get the wine you like."

"Then I appreciate it. I haven't been able to have it very often."

"You're welcome. Why don't you make yourself comfortable, and I'll start dinner?"

I nodded, but instead of sitting down, I set my wine glass on the island and went around to the other side. He turned to me and pulled me into his arms.

"This isn't getting comfortable," he murmured.

"I haven't kissed you yet tonight."

"Mmm, I can see how that would improve your comfort levels." He leaned down and pressed his lips against mine, kissing me deeply, but with an affection that couldn't be denied.

We broke apart, and I found myself smiling widely. "Okay, I'm ready for dinner now."

He chuckled. "Coming right up."

"And I hope it's okay, but I completely forgot my pyjamas."

"I think that'll be just fine," he responded.

I hopped onto the chair on the other side of the island, enjoying how calm and settled this felt, even if we hadn't known one another long.

Sometimes, not long was all it took.

EIGHT

ANISE

THE SOFT SOUNDS of morning woke me and I stretched across the bed, confused for a moment about why it didn't feel like mine until I remembered where I was.

I smiled sleepily and turned onto my side, reaching out my arm and hoping to find Kuk next to me. But his side of the bed was empty, though it was still warm from where he'd been sleeping.

A light breeze came from the other side of the room, and I sat up, only then realising that there was a balcony attached to his bedroom. I supposed I hadn't had much time to look around when we'd fallen into his bed in a tangle of limbs.

It was hard to believe he had a balcony, but it actually fitted with the rest of the room. It was spacious and neatly decorated, with an en-suite bathroom that I was sure we'd be putting to good use soon.

I wasn't going to lie, if we continued dating, then I was definitely going to get used to this. And if we ended up moving in together, then it was *definitely* going to be into his place and not mine.

The curtain drifted open with the wind, and I spotted a lone figure outside. I guessed that answered where Kuk had gotten to.

I threw back the covers and grabbed his shirt from where it had landed last night, pulling it on, but only buttoning a few. No one who bought a flat like this wouldn't have given a thought to privacy when on the balcony.

I made my way over, enjoying the quiet that came with the early morning. I pushed open the glass door and stepped outside.

Kuk turned, smiling when he saw me. "I didn't mean to wake you."

"You didn't."

He reached out and pulled me into his arms, kissing me gently.

"I like your outfit," he murmured when we broke the kiss.

"I call it *Anise the morning after.*"

He chuckled. "I'd like to see it in more colours."

"Then you should keep inviting me over for dinner."

"Done." His voice rumbled as he said the word and I knew he wasn't just saying it. He meant everything he was saying to me.

I smiled widely. "Why are you out here?" I asked.

"I came out to enjoy the dawn," he responded.

"I thought you wouldn't like it?"

"Because I'm the god of darkness?" he asked curiously.

"Well, yes. I don't know how this god thing works." Though I was starting to realise that it *wasn't* the way I thought it was.

"I see your research wasn't quite as thorough as you'd like," he responded. "I'm specifically the god of the darkness at dawn. Well, and obscurity. My sister is the goddess of the darkness at dusk. And obscurity too, we share that one."

"Ah. I hadn't realised there was a difference."

"We're conflated in some myths," he said. "I think that's caused some confusion about it."

"Huh. But you're definitely different people, right?"

"Would it be a problem if we weren't?" He gave me a curious look.

I frowned. Would it? "I don't know, I haven't met your sister, so that might be a bit weird. But I'm sure I'd feel differently once I have."

He snorted "I'm not sure about that, Kuaket is a force to be reckoned with. But no, we're not the same person. Thankfully. I don't think I'd be able to deal with her in my head all the time."

"I'm sure she's not that bad."

"She's my twin sister, we share a connection that thousands of years hasn't shaken, but we're different people."

"So day-night and night-night," I quipped.

He groaned. "You have to know that was a bad joke."

"It was terrible, but there was a part of you that thought it was funny too."

"Hmm." He kissed the top of my head.

I leaned into him and let out a satisfied sigh. "I've never noticed how beautiful the sky is just before dawn."

"Could that be because you've rarely been awake at this time?" he asked.

"Almost certainly," I responded. "But even so, it's beautiful. And it does feel like you."

He raised an eyebrow.

"It's calm, but every time you look back at it, you find new levels to it. The colours and the sounds. It's like this whole thing with different layers that makes up the whole. It does make me think of you."

"I see."

"It's steady."

"And you think I'm steady?" He sounded surprised, though I wasn't entirely sure why that might be. I hadn't known him long, but I already knew that he was.

"Yes. Which is weird. We barely know each other still. I mean, you know me in ways that a lot of people don't, but it still feels that way," I assured him, hoping he realised how much truth there was in my thoughts.

He nodded. "I feel that way around you too, like this is something."

"It is. I plan on staying around for a long time to come. If you'll have me, of course."

"Definitely." He pulled me closer and pressed his lips against mine.

I melted into the kiss, enjoying the way it felt for

my body to be against his and trying not to recall too many memories of the night before as I did.

Kuk broke the kiss and scooped me up into his arms, making me laugh in the process.

"What are you doing?" I asked through my laughter.

"Taking you back to bed." His voice rumbled through me, making my whole body tingle.

"But you're out here."

"I was planning on coming with you." Promise dripped through every word and I tried not to let out a whimper in response.

From the expression on his face, I was reasonably certain he'd noticed it.

"Oh." I trailed my hand across his bare chest, able to feel every beat of his heart as he carried me back inside and laid me back on the bed.

I pulled him with me, ready to lose myself in the connection we were forging. With every moment I spent with him, every touch, every kiss, and every word, I could feel what we had growing.

And all it had taken to find him was one lucky swipe right.

EPILOGUE

ANISE

THE DOOR to the Coven Copy Shop swung open and I looked up, hoping that it was Kuk coming to pick me up now my shift had ended, but no such luck for me. At least he'd be here soon and we could disappear back into our own world.

Chelsea, on the other hand, was hurrying over to Baal, clearly as enamoured as the first time he came into the shop. Only this time, she knew he was interested in her. I still hadn't gotten the full story about what had happened at the photo shoot he'd asked for her help at, which was a shame because apparently, it had involved naked gods. I was sure I'd manage to get it at some point.

"Hey, Anise," he said, waving to me even as he put an arm around Chelsea.

"Hi. How's it going?" I responded, flashing him a friendly smile.

"Good, I think. I'm just taking Chelsea to do a shoot at Horus' sanctuary."

"So we're just dropping all pretence that you guys aren't gods then, huh?" I joked.

"It was never meant to be a secret from you, I actually assumed that you knew." He shrugged.

I supposed that was fair. Kuk had told me he was a god as soon as he'd realised I was paranormal myself, I suspected Baal would have done the same if Chelsea had asked him what he was.

"I only looked you up because Anise suggested it," Chelsea responded. "I really should have done that sooner."

"I'm glad you didn't," Baal said, kissing her cheek. "I enjoyed how we got together."

Chelsea flushed furiously, and I had to wonder exactly what was causing that response, but I didn't pry. She'd either tell me in her own time, or she'd keep it to herself. Who was I to judge? I hadn't told her the exact ins and outs of what had gone on with me and Kuk yet, just that we'd met on a dating app.

The door opened and my heart skipped a beat at the sight of the handsome god entering. Baal might be here for Chelsea, but Kuk was here for me.

The other two turned in the direction of the newcomer and surprised recognition flitted over Baal's face.

"Hey, Baal," Kuk said cheerily, not seeming in the slightest bit confused by who he was.

Which made sense. They were both gods and lived in the same city. Kuk had even talked about Baal with me, they clearly knew one another and I'd just never put the pieces properly together.

"I didn't expect to see you here," Baal responded as the two of them did the weird back-slapping-man-hello with one another.

"I'm here to pick up Anise," Kuk said.

Understanding dawned in Baal's eyes. "Ah, she's the girlfriend."

Kuk nodded and brushed his hand against the small of my back.

A thrill rushed through me, both at the show of affection, and his casual acknowledgement of me as his girlfriend.

"Hey, I've been meaning to tell you, I'm sorry I couldn't do your calendar. Kua said it went great," Kuk said.

"It did, mostly thanks to Chelsea's assistance."

My friend snorted. "Hardly. You'd have done just fine without me."

"Except that without you, I'd only have been able to shoot eleven gods," he pointed out.

"You'd have found another replacement for Fenrir," she mumbled, though I could tell from her face that she was happy about the recognition from him. His actions at the photo shoot had probably made a huge difference to her budding career as a photographer. No doubt she would end up leaving the Coven Copy Shop before the end of the year. I was going to miss her, but it would be worth it to see her flourish.

Kuk took my hand in his, causing a warm surge of affection to flood through me. I was still getting used to having someone around who treated me this way.

I looked at him out of the corner of my eye and smiled, getting one back in return.

"Right, we'd better get going or we'll be late for our reservation," Kuk said.

"Yep, I'm all yours," I said, grabbing my bag from behind the counter. "I'll see you tomorrow, Chelsea."

She waved us off, and the two of us left the shop hand-in-hand. The moment we were around the corner, Kuk tugged on my hand and pulled me in.

He brushed my hair out of my face and smoothed his thumb over my cheek.

"Hey," he whispered.

"Hi. It's good to see you."

"It always is," he responded, leaning in.

Despite the fact we'd kissed dozens of times by this point, I could feel the tension hanging in the air, the promise of what it would feel like when he pressed his lips against mine.

I closed the short distance between us and kissed him deeply. He returned it instantly and I lost myself in everything that was us and the future that we were going to build. The one I became more certain of with each passing day.

Our kiss ended, but we didn't pull apart. Kuk leaned his forehead against mine and I found myself looking into his earnest gaze.

"I love you, Anise," he whispered.

My breathing hitched at the words. I hadn't expected to hear him say them so soon, even if I was already certain he felt them.

But there they were, out in the open. For one horrible moment, I thought they'd make me panic, but they didn't. Instead, they settled deep within me and gave me the courage to put a voice to my own feelings.

"I love you too, Kuk."

As soon as the words left my mouth, they solidified something, and I knew that there was no going back from this.

Not that I wanted to. I could tell I had a future with Kuk, and I was looking forward to building it.

* * *

THANK you for reading *Matching A Dawn God*, I hope you enjoyed it! If you want more from the *To Date A God* series, then you can start the series with *Dating A Love Goddess*: http://books2read.com/datingalovegoddess

Or, if you want to find out more about Chelsea and Baal, you can check out their story here: http://books2read.com/baaldenizens

AUTHOR NOTE

Thank you for reading *Matching A Dawn God*, I hope you enjoyed it!

I've wanted to write a story for Kuk (and ultimately for Kuaket) for a while, ever since I made a joint version of them an antagonist in *Protectors Of Poison* (part of my *Forgotten Gods* series, which is also based on mythology but is set in a different universe). While they were antagonists there, I never saw the god/goddess pairing themselves as bad, so wanted to give them a story where they could be the ones with the happy ever afters! In this universe, I did split them up into two characters, which is partly to differentiate them, but also because sometimes they are considered two sides of one deity, and sometimes they are considered two. I felt like having them one way in one universe, and another in the other, was a good way of paying homage to that. The mythology of Kuk being the god of the dark at dawn, and Kuaket the goddess of the dark at dusk is genuine Egyptian mythology, and I kept it in as I thought it was good at displaying how different the twins are from one another.

You can find Chelsea and Baal's romance in *Baal*, where Chelsea helps Baal with a photo shoot to make a naked gods calendar, and the two of them realise just how they feel about one another. You can also find several of the other gods mentioned in books of their own - including Bastet in *Bastet*, where she reconnects with Ptah, her ex. And you can find Seth and Menhit in *Seth*. You can also find Horus in *Horus* where he connects with a new vet working at his animal sanctuary.

Kuk's sister, Kuaket, will also have a story of her own, one that reveals the complications of her relationship with the warlock she shouldn't be dating.

If you want more from the *To Date A God* universe, you can start the series with *Dating A Love Goddess*, which follows a Celtic love goddess and an Egyptian love god as they try to work out if they can work together.

If you want more romance with the dating app

connection, I'd recommend heading towards *Seth*, which involves a mistaken identity situation between Menhit and Seth, two gods who don't realise who they're talking to. It's set in the same world as *Matching A Dawn God*! Or you can try the *MatchMater Paranormal Dating App* sub-series of *The Paranormal Council*, which follows various paranormals as they find their fated mates via a dating app.

If you want to keep up to date with new releases and other news, you can join my Facebook Reader Group or mailing list.

Stay safe & happy reading!

- Laura

ALSO BY LAURA GREENWOOD

You can find out more about each of my series on my website.

Obscure Academy

A paranormal romance series set at a university-age academy for mixed supernaturals. Each book follows a different couple.

The Apprentice Of Anubis

An urban fantasy series set in an alternative world where the Ancient Egyptian Empire never fell. It follows a new apprentice to the temple of Anubis as she learns about her new role.

Forgotten Gods

A paranormal adventure romance series inspired by Egyptian mythology. Each book follows a different Ancient Egyptian goddess.

Amethyst's Wand Shop Mysteries (with Arizona Tape)

An urban fantasy murder mystery series following a witch who teams up with a detective to solve murders. Each book includes a different murder.

Grimm Academy

A fantasy fairy tale academy series. Each book follows a different fairy tale heroine.

Jinx Paranormal Dating Agency

A paranormal romance series based on worldwide mythology where paranormals and deities take part in events organised by the Jinx Dating Agency. Each book follows a different couple.

Purple Oasis (with Arizona Tape)

A paranormal romance series based at a sanctuary set up after the apocalypse. Each book follows a different couple.

Speed Dating With The Denizens Of The Underworld (shared world)

A paranormal romance shared world based on mythology from around the world. Each book follows a different couple.

Blackthorn Academy For Supernaturals

A paranormal monster romance shared world based at Blackthorn Academy. Each book follows a different couple.

You can find a complete list of all my books on my

website:

https://www.authorlauragreenwood.co.uk/p/book-list.html

Signed Paperback & Merchandise:

You can find signed paperbacks, hardcovers, and merchandise based on my series (including stickers, magnets, face masks, and more!) via my website: https://www.authorlauragreenwood.co.uk/p/shop.html

ABOUT LAURA GREENWOOD

Laura is a USA Today Bestselling Author of paranormal romance, urban fantasy, and fantasy romance. When she's not writing, she drinks a lot of tea, tries to resist French macarons, and works towards a diploma in Egyptology. She lives in the UK, where most of her books are set. Laura specialises in quick reads, with healthy relationships and consent positive moments regardless of if she's writing light-hearted romance, mythology-heavy urban fantasy, or anything in between.

Follow Laura Greenwood

- Website: https://www. authorlauragreenwood.co.uk
- Mailing List: https://www. authorlauragreenwood.co.uk/p/book-sign-up.html
- Facebook Group: https://facebook.com/ groups/theparanormalcouncil

- Facebook Page: https://facebook.com/authorlauragreenwood
- Bookbub: https://bookbub.com/authors/laura-greenwood

Milton Keynes UK
Ingram Content Group UK Ltd.
UKHW041842090224
437425UK00006B/116